Anima

A FABLE IN TWO ACTS

Adapted by Nelson Bond

from the book
by George Orwell

SAMUEL FRENCH, INC.
45 WEST 25TH STREET   NEW YORK 10010
7623 SUNSET BOULEVARD HOLLYWOOD 90046
LONDON   TORONTO

STORY OF THE PLAY

George Orwell's biting satire, adapted by Nelson Bond. *Animal Farm* is a fable with a sting. Millions of words have been written about the threat of Totalitarianism, but it remained to the late George Orwell, farsighted British author of the brilliant and frightening *1984,* to expose the Russian experiment for what it really is: an idealist's dream, converted by realists into a nightmare. In Nelson Bond's simply staged dramatic reading version of this timely allegory you will meet beasts whose prototypes have dominated news headlines for a half hundred fearful years. Opening on a note of joyous triumph for the creatures who have emancipated themselves from the cruel mastery of a human owner, the reading mounts inexorably to a climax of disillusionment in which the other animals discover themselves now subject to the rule of even more ruthless autocrats: the greedy, cunning pigs. "Intermingling humor and drama, *Animal Farm* wrings the emotions of its listeners, leaving audiences shaken with the tale of a tragedy that happened in a mythical barnyard far away, but could . . . if we denizens of a finer and more modern farm are content to languish in bovine complacency . . . most terribly and swiftly happen in our own back yard."

ANIMAL FARM was first presented at The Show-timers Studio Theatre, Roanoke, Virginia, on September 29, 1961. The play was directed and produced by the adapter, Nelson Bond, with the following cast:

NARRATOR ....*Francis Ballard*

STOOL No. 2 ....*Jim Ayers*

STOOL No. 3 ....*Robert W. Ayers*

STOOL No. 4 ....*Evaline Youse*

STOOL No. 5 ....*Ben B. Dulaney*

STOOL No. 6 ....*Art Glover*

STOOL No. 7 ....*Virginia Holton*

NOTE

No actual props are used in the production of ANIMAL FARM. All physical actions are indicated by the actors through pantomime.

CAST OF CHARACTERS

Each of the Readers has one principal role with which he is identified, and one or more minor roles. In addition, each Reader from time to time serves as a Narrator, and thus aids the principal Narrator in progressing the story.

Stool No. 1 ....NARRATOR
JONES

Stool No. 2 ....SNOWBALL
BENJAMIN

Stool No. 3 ....SQUEALER
MOSES
FREDERICK

Stool No. 4 ....CLOVER
CAT

Stool No. 5 ....BOXER
PILKINGTON

Stool No. 6 ....MAJOR
NAPOLEON

Stool No. 7 ....MOLLIE
MURIEL

The entire action of the reading takes place in England . . . according to the author. You may decide for yourself that the real scene is set several hundreds of miles farther to the east. The time is, most regrettably, the present.

A WORD ABOUT DRAMATIC READINGS

Readings are at once the oldest and the newest form of dramatic entertainment. The roots of this art lie deep in the history of civilization, dating back to an era when only a favored few were lettered, and shared their good fortune with the masses by reading aloud great stories, plays and poems.

Recent years have seen a renascence of interest in this rich interpretative medium. The stage, TV, and movies notwithstanding, there are innumerable tales so wide in scope, spanning such vast periods of space and time, that their events cannot adequately be portrayed by settings. Such vistas can only be encompassed by the mind, wherein the limitless canvas of the imagination can be painted by the words and voices of the readers.

Dramatic readings require skill on the part of the narrators, and on the part of the listeners demand that wondrous quality of acceptance which Coleridge called "the willing suspension of disbelief." Therefore, to enjoy tonight's performance, simply close your eyes and let the readers' voices carry you away to a time, a space, you did not know you knew.

Animal Farm

ACT I

As the house lights lower, Music Cue No. 1 *begins. After the music has established, the curtains part on an empty stage, dimly illuminated by the holding lights on the reading stands. The six readers occupying Stools 2 through 7 enter and seat themselves. When they are seated, the principal* NARRATOR *(Stool 1) enters, moves swiftly to his stool and turns on his reading light. As the music ends, he begins reading. (Numbers in front of character names are the stool numbers.)*

1 JONES. Mr. Jones, of the Manor Farm, was drunk! He lurched across the yard, kicked off his boots at the back door, drew himself a last glass of beer from the barrel in the scullery, and made his way up to bed.

4 NARRATOR. As soon as the light went out there was a stirring and a fluttering all through the farm buildings.

6 MAJOR. Word had gone round that old Major, the prize boar, had had a strange dream, and wished to communicate it to the other animals as soon as Mr. Jones was safely out of the way.

5 NARRATOR. Old Major was so highly regarded that everyone was quite ready to lose an hour's sleep in order to hear what he had to say.

2 NARRATOR. First came the dogs, then the pigs, who settled down in the straw immediately in front of the platform.

7 NARRATOR. The hens perched themselves on the windowsills, the pigeons fluttered up to the rafters, the sheep and cows lay down behind the pigs and began to chew the cud.

3 NARRATOR. The two cart-horses, Boxer and Clover, came in together, setting down their vast, hairy hoofs with great care, lest there should be some small animal concealed in the straw.

4 CLOVER. Clover was a stout, motherly mare who had never quite got back her figure after her fourth foal.

5 BOXER. Boxer was an enormous beast nearly eighteen hands high, as strong as any two ordinary horses put together. He was not of first-rate intelligence, but he was universally respected for his steadiness of character and tremendous powers of work.

4 NARRATOR. After the horses came Muriel, the goat, and Benjamin, the donkey. Benjamin was the oldest animal on the farm . . . and the worst tempered. He seldom talked, and when he did it was usually to make some cynical remark, such as:

2 BENJAMIN. God gave me a tail to keep the flies off. But I'd rather have had no tail . . . and no flies!

7 MOLLIE. At the last moment, Mollie, the foolish, pretty white mare who drew Mr. Jones' trap, came mincing daintily in, flirting her mane to draw attention to the red ribbons it was plaited with.

1 NARRATOR. All the animals now being present, Major cleared his throat and began:

6 MAJOR. Comrades, you have heard about the strange dream I had last night. But I have something else to tell you about first. I do not think, comrades, I shall be with you very much longer . . .

ALL. Oh, no, Major! No!

6 MAJOR. (*Over them.*) And before I die, I feel it my duty to pass on to you such wisdom as I have acquired. I have had a long life, and think I understand the nature of life on this earth as well as any animal now living. It is about this I wish to speak to you. Now, comrades, what is the nature of this life of ours? Let us face it . . . our lives are miserable, laborious and short. We are given just so much food as will keep the breath in our bodies, are forced to work to the last atom of our strength . . .

and the moment our usefulness has come to an end, we are slaughtered with hideous cruelty.

2 BENJAMIN. Isn't this simply part of the order of nature?

4 CLOVER. Isn't it because this land is so poor?

6 MAJOR. No, comrades! A thousand times, no! This farm of ours would support a dozen horses, twenty cows, hundreds of sheep, in a comfort and dignity almost beyond our imagining!

3 SQUEALER. Then why do we continue in this miserable condition?

6 MAJOR. Because the produce of our labor is stolen from us. Comrades, the answer to all of our problems lies in a single word . . . Man! Man is the only creature that consumes without producing.

1 ANIMAL. True! He does not give milk . . .

4 ANIMAL. He does not lay eggs . . .

5 BOXER. He is too weak to pull a plough . . .

6 MAJOR. Yet he is the lord of all the animals. He sets us to work, gives back the bare minimum that will keep us from starving . . . and keeps the rest for himself.

5 BOXER. *Our* labor tills the soil.

2 BENJAMIN. *Our* dung fertilizes it.

7 MOLLIE. Yet there is not one of us that owns more than his own skin!

6 MAJOR. Even the miserable lives we lead are not allowed to reach their natural span. No animal escapes the cruel knife in the end. You young porkers sitting in front of me . . . within a year, every one of you will scream your lives out at the block. To that horror we must all come . . . cows, pigs, hens, everyone!

ALL. No! No! Oh, no!

5 BOXER. Even the horses?

6 MAJOR. You, Boxer . . . the day those great muscles of yours lose their power, Jones will sell you to the knacker, who will cut your throat and boil you down into glue.

4 CLOVER. What, then, must we do?

6 MAJOR. Why, work, night and day, body and soul,

for the overthrow of the human race! That is my message to you, comrades. Rebellion!

ALL. (*Firmly.*) Rebellion! (*Uncertainly.*) Rebellion?

6 MAJOR. Rebellion! Fix your eyes on that, comrades. Never listen when they tell you Man and the animals have a common interest. Man serves the interest of no creature except himself. Whatever goes on two legs is an enemy. Whatever goes on four legs, or has wings, is a friend.

ALL. All animals are friends! Down with Humanity!

6 MAJOR. And remember that in fighting Man we must not come to resemble him. No animal must ever live in a house, or sleep in a bed, or wear clothes, or drink alcohol, or smoke tobacco, or engage in trade. Above all, no animal must ever tyrannize over his own kind. Weak or strong, clever or simple, we are all brothers. No animal must ever kill any other animal. All animals are equal!

ALL. All animals are equal! All animals are brothers!

6 MAJOR. And now, comrades, I will tell you about my dream. It was a dream of the earth as it will be when Man has vanished. Many years ago, when I was a little pig, my mother used to sing an old song. Last night in my dream the words of that song came back . . . words sung by the animals of long ago, and lost to memory for generations. I will sing that song now, comrades. I am old, and my voice is hoarse. But when I have taught you the tune you can sing it better for yourselves. It is called . . . "Beasts of England." (*Music Cue No. 2. Sings.*)

> Beasts of England, Beasts of Ireland,
> Beasts of every land and clime,
> Hearken to my joyful tidings
> Of the golden future time.

1 & 7. (*Join in.*)

> Soon or late the day is coming
> Tyrant Man shall be o'erthrown,
> And the fruitful fields of England
> Shall be trod by beasts alone.

4 & 5. (*Join in.*)

> Rings shall vanish from our noses,

And the harness from our back,
Bit and spur shall rust forever,
Cruel whips no more shall crack.

2 & 3. (*Join in.*)

Bright will shine the fields of England,
Purer shall its waters be,
Sweeter yet shall blow the breezes
On the day that sets us free.

ALL.

Beasts of England, beasts of Ireland,
Beasts of every land and clime,
Hearken well and spread my tidings
Of the golden future time.

(All continue to hum softly under:)

1 NARRATOR. Before Major had reached the end, even the stupidest of them had picked up the tune. The whole farm burst into "Beasts of England" in tremendous unison. The cows lowed it, the dogs whined it, the ducks quacked it. They were so delighted with the song that they might have continued singing all night. Unfortunately the uproar woke Mr. Jones, who sprang out of bed, seized the gun which stood in the corner of his bedroom, and let fly a charge of Number 6 shot into the darkness. The meeting broke up hurriedly!

(The music breaks off abruptly. After a pause we hear Music Cue No. 3, which fades under:)

7 NARRATOR. Old Major died early in March. During the next three months there was much secret activity. Major's speech had given the animals a completely new outlook on life. They did not know *when* the predicted Rebellion would take place, but they saw it was their duty to prepare for it.

1 NARRATOR. The work of organizing fell naturally on the pigs, who were generally recognized as being the cleverest of the animals. Pre-eminent among the pigs were two named Snowball and Napoleon.

6 NAPOLEON. Napoleon was a large, fierce-looking Berkshire boar with a reputation for getting his own way.

2 SNOWBALL. Snowball was a more vivacious pig, quicker in speech and more inventive . . .

6 NAPOLEON. . . . but not considered to have the same depth of character!

3 SQUEALER. All the other male pigs on the farm were porkers. The best known among them was a small, fat pig named Squealer . . . a brilliant talker, and very persuasive.

1 NARRATOR. These three elaborated old Major's teachings into a complete system of thought to which they gave the name Animalism. Several nights a week they held secret meetings in the barn and expounded the principles of Animalism to the others. At the beginning, they met with much stupidity and apathy.

7 MOLLIE. We should be loyal to Mr. Jones. He's our Master!

4 CLOVER. Besides, he feeds us. If he were gone, wouldn't we starve to death?

2 BENJAMIN. Why should we care what happens after we're dead?

4 BOXER. If this Rebellion is going to happen anyway, what difference whether we work for it or not?

1 NARRATOR. The stupidest questions of all were asked by Mollie, the white mare.

7 MOLLIE. (*To* NAPOLEON.) Will there still be sugar after the Rebellion?

6 NAPOLEON. You do not need sugar. You will have all the hay and oats you want.

7 MOLLIE. And shall I still be allowed to wear ribbons in my hair?

6 NAPOLEON. Comrade, those ribbons you are so devoted to are the badge of slavery. Can't you understand that liberty is worth more than ribbons?

1 NARRATOR. Mollie agreed, but she did not sound very convinced. The pigs had an even harder time attempting to counteract the lies put out by Moses, the

raven. Moses, who was Mr. Jones' special pet, claimed to know of the existence of a mysterious country called . . .

3 MOSES. (*Raptly.*) Sugarcandy Mountain! Oh, Sugarcandy Mountain, brethren . . . that wondrous land to which all good animals go when they depart this vale of tears! It lies 'way up there in the sky, dearly beloved, a little distance beyond the clouds. On Sugarcandy Mountain clover is in season all year round . . . lump sugar and linseed cake grow on the hedges. Oh, hallelujah, brethren . . . be joyous for the day when we shall all see Sugarcandy Mountain!

1 NARRATOR. The animals hated Moses because he did no work. But most of them believed in Sugarcandy Mountain, and the pigs had to argue very hard to persuade them there was no such place.

7 NARRATOR. The most faithful disciples were the two horses, Boxer and Clover. These two had great difficulty in thinking anything out for themselves. But once having accepted the pigs as their teachers, they absorbed everything they were told, and led the singing of "Beasts of England" with which the meetings always ended.

4 & 5. All together, now! (*Sing.*) Beasts of England, beasts of Ireland, beasts of every land and clime . . .

1 NARRATOR. Now, as it turned out, the Rebellion came about much earlier than anyone had expected. On Midsummer's Eve, Mr. Jones got so drunk that he went to sleep on the drawing-room sofa with a newspaper over his face. When evening came, the animals were still unfed.

4 ANIMAL. At last they could stand it no longer. One of the cows broke in the door of the store shed, and all the animals began to help themselves from the bins.

1 JONES. Just then Mr. Jones woke up. The next moment, he and four of his men were in the store shed with whips, lashing out in all directions.

2 ANIMAL. This was more than the hungry animals could bear. Though nothing of the kind had been planned, they flung themselves upon their tormentors.

1 JONES. Jones and his men suddenly found themselves being butted and kicked from all sides. This sudden up-

rising of creatures they were used to thrashing and mal-
treating frightened them almost out of their wits. They
took to their heels. A minute later all five of them were
in full flight down the road, with the animals crying after
them:

ALL. (*Shout.*) Get out! And *stay* out!

7 NARRATOR. And so, almost before the animals knew
what was happening, the Rebellion had been successfully
carried through. Jones was expelled, and the Manor Farm
was theirs.

3 NARRATOR. Their first act was to wipe out the last
traces of Jones' hated reign. The harness room was broken
open. The bits, the nose rings, the cruel knives Mr. Jones
had used to castrate the pigs and lambs, all were flung
down the well.

6 NARRATOR. The reins, the halters, the blinkers, and
the degrading nosebags were thrown on the rubbish fire.
So were the whips.

1 NARRATOR. Snowball also threw onto the fire the ribbons with which the horses' manes and tails had been
decorated on market days, explaining:

2 SNOWBALL. Ribbons should be considered as clothes,
which are a mark of the human being. All animals should
go naked.

5 BOXER. When Boxer heard this, he fetched the small
straw hat he wore in summer to keep the flies out of his
ears, and flung it on the fire with the rest.

7 NARRATOR. In a very little while the animals had
destroyed everything that reminded them of Mr. Jones.
Then they filed back to the farmhouse and halted outside
the door.

2 SNOWBALL. After a moment, Snowball and Napoleon
butted the door open and the animals entered. They tiptoed from room to room, gazing with a kind of awe at
the unbelievable luxury . . . at the beds with their
feather mattresses, the looking-glasses, the sofa made of
horsehair, the Brussels carpet, the lithograph of Queen
Victoria over the drawing-room mantelpiece.

7 MOLLIE. As they were coming down the stairs, Mollie

was discovered to be missing. Going back, the others found her in the best bedroom. She had taken a piece of blue ribbon from Mrs. Jones' dressing-table, and was holding it against her shoulder, admiring herself in the glass.

1 NARRATOR. The other reproached her sharply and went outside. Some hams hanging in the kitchen were taken out for burial. A unanimous resolution was passed on the spot that the farmhouse should be preserved as a museum. All agreed that no animal must ever live there.

7 NARRATOR. The next day Snowball and Napoleon called them all together again and revealed that during the past three months the pigs had taught themselves to read and write.

6 NAPOLEON. Napoleon sent for pots of paint, and led the way to the gate that gave onto the main road.

2 SNOWBALL. Snowball painted out the name Manor Farm from the top bar of the gate, and in its place painted Animal Farm.

7 NARRATOR. After this, they went back to the farm buildings, where Snowball and Napoleon set a ladder against the end wall of the big barn. They explained that the pigs had succeeded in reducing the principles of Animalism to Seven Commandments. These would now be inscribed on the wall, and would form an unalterable law by which all the animals on Animal Farm must live forever after.

2 SNOWBALL. With some difficulty (for it is not easy for a pig to balance himself on a ladder) Snowball climbed up and set to work. The Commandments were written on the wall in great white letters.

4 CLOVER. Whatever goes upon two legs is an enemy.

5 BOXER. Whatever goes upon four legs, or has wings, is a friend.

6 NAPOLEON. No animal shall wear clothes.

7 MURIEL. No animal shall sleep in a bed.

1 ANIMAL. No animal shall drink alcohol.

2 SNOWBALL. No animal shall kill any other animal.

3 CLOVER. All animals are equal.

7 NARRATOR. It was all very neatly written . . . except that one of the S's was the wrong way round. Snowball read it aloud. All the animals nodded in complete agreement, and the cleverer ones at once began to learn the Commandments by heart.

1 NARRATOR. But at this moment the three cows set up a loud lowing. They had not been milked for hours, and their udders were bursting. The pigs sent for buckets, and milked the cows fairly successfully. Soon there were five buckets of frothing, creamy milk, at which many of the animals looked with considerable interest.

4 CAT. What's going to happen to all that milk?

5 BOXER. Jones used to mix some of it in our mash.

6 NAPOLEON. Never mind the milk, comrades. The harvest is more important. Comrade Snowball will lead the way. I shall follow in a few minutes. Forward, comrades! The hay is waiting!

1 NARRATOR. So the animals trooped down to the hayfield to begin the harvest. And when they came back in the evening, it was noticed that the milk had disappeared.

(Music Cue No. 4.)

7 NARRATOR. How they toiled and sweated to get the hay in! But their efforts were rewarded, for the harvest was an even bigger success than they had hoped.

6 NAPOLEON. The work was hard. The implements had been designed for human beings, and no animal was able to use any tool that involved standing on his hind legs. But the pigs were so clever that they could think of a way around every difficulty.

4 CLOVER. The pigs did not actually work, but supervised the others. Boxer and Clover would harness themselves to the cutter or horse-rake (no bits or reins were needed, of course), and tramp steadily around and around the field with a pig walking beside and calling out:

3 SQUEALER. Gee there, comrade! Whoa there, comrade!

7 NARRATOR. Every animal down to the humblest

worked. Even the ducks and hens toiled to and fro carrying tiny wisps of hay in their beaks. In the end, they finished the harvest in two days less time than it had usually taken Jones and his men. Moreover, it was the biggest harvest the farm had ever seen.

1 NARRATOR. All that summer the work of the farm went like clockwork. The animals were happy as they had never conceived it possible to be. Every mouthful of food was a positive pleasure now that it was truly their own food, produced by themselves and for themselves.

5 BOXER. Boxer was the admiration of everybody. From morning to night he was always at the spot where the work was hardest. He had made arrangements with one of the cockerels to call him in the mornings half an hour earlier than anyone else, and would labor at whatever seemed most needed before the regular day's work began. His personal motto was, "I will work harder!"

7 MOLLIE. Nobody shirked . . . or almost nobody. Mollie would vanish for hours, then reappear at mealtimes. But she always had such excellent excuses that it was impossible not to believe in her good intentions.

1 NARRATOR. Only old Benjamin, the donkey, seemed quite unchanged. He did his work in the same slow, obstinate way as in Jones' time, never shirking, and never volunteering for extra work, either. About the Rebellion he would express no opinion. When asked whether he was not happier now that Jones was gone, he would only say cryptically:

2 BENJAMIN. Nobody's ever seen a dead donkey!

7 NARRATOR. On Sundays all the animals trooped into the big barn for a general assembly. Here the work of the coming week was planned, and resolutions were debated. It was always the pigs who put forward the resolutions. The other animals could not think of any. Snowball and Napoleon were by far the most active in the debates. But it was noticed that whatever suggestion either of them made, the other could be counted on to oppose it.

2 SNOWBALL. Snowball busied himself organizing committees. He formed the Egg Production Committee for

the hens, the Clean Tails Committee for the cows, and the Wild Comrades Re-education Committee. The object of this last was to tame the rats and rabbits, but the project broke down almost immediately.

4 CAT. The cat joined the Re-education Committee, and was very active in it . . . for a while. She was seen one day sitting on a roof and talking to some sparrows who were just out of her reach. She was telling them that all animals were now comrades, and that any sparrow who chose could come and perch on her paw. But the sparrows kept their distance.

1 NARRATOR. By autumn, almost every animal on the farm was literate to some degree. The pigs could read and write perfectly. The dogs learned to read fairly well. Muriel, the goat, could read somewhat better than the dogs. Benjamin could read as well as any pig, but never exercised his faculty. He said:

2 BENJAMIN. Far as I can see, there's nothing worth reading!

4 CLOVER. Clover learned the whole alphabet, but she could never put words together.

5 BOXER. Boxer couldn't get beyond the letter D. He would trace out A, B, C, D in the dust with his hoof, then stand staring at the letters, trying with all his might to remember what came next. On several occasions he did learn E, F, G, H. But by the time he knew them, he had forgotten A, B, C and D.

7 MOLLIE. Mollie refused to learn any but the letters which spelt her own name. She would form these very neatly out of pieces of twig, then decorate them with a flower or two and walk around them, admiring them.

1 NARRATOR. None of the other animals could get farther than the letter A. It was also found that the stupider animals, such as the sheep, hens and ducks, were unable to learn the Seven Commandments by heart. After much thought, Snowball solved this problem.

2 SNOWBALL. Comrades, for your benefit I have reduced the Seven Commandments to a single maxim. Listen carefully. "Four legs good; two legs bad. Four legs

good; two legs bad." Now, repeat after me. Four legs
good . . .

ALL. Four legs good . . .

2 SNOWBALL. Two legs bad.

ALL. Two legs bad.

2 SNOWBALL. Excellent! Now, all together once more!

ALL. Four legs . . .

2 SNOWBALL. (*Prompting.*) Good.

ALL. Good. Two legs . . .

2 SNOWBALL. Bad.

ALL. Two legs bad.

2 SNOWBALL. Now, once again.

ALL. (*With increasing confidence.*) Four legs, good;
two legs, bad. Four legs, good; two legs, bad.

1 NARRATOR. This maxim was inscribed on the wall of
the barn above the Seven Commandments. Once they had
it by heart, the sheep developed a great liking for the
maxim, and often as they lay in the field would all start
bleating:

ALL. Four legs good; two legs bad. Four legs good; two
legs baaad. Four legs good; two legs baaaaad!

1 NARRATOR. (*Up, over them.*) And keep it up for
hours on end!

6 NAPOLEON. Napoleon took no interest in Snowball's
committees. He said education of the young was more important. Two farm dogs had whelped soon after the harvest, giving birth to nine sturdy puppies. As soon as they
were weaned, Napoleon took them, saying he would make
himself responsible for their education. He took them to a
loft over the harness room, and there kept them in such
seclusion that the rest of the animals quite forgot their
existence.

1 NARRATOR. The mystery of where the milk went to
was soon cleared up. It was mixed every day into the
pigs' mash. The early apples were now ripening, and the
orchard was littered with windfalls. The animals had assumed these would be shared equally. One day, however,
the order went forth that all windfalls were to be brought
to the harness-room for the use of the pigs. At this, some

of the other animals murmured. Squealer was sent to make the necessary explanations.

3 SQUEALER. Comrades, surely you do not imagine we pigs are doing this in a spirit of selfishness or privilege? Many of us actually *dislike* milk and apples! Our sole object is to preserve our health. Milk and apples . . . this has been proven by Science, comrades! . . . contain substances absolutely necessary to the well-being of a pig. We pigs are brain workers. The whole management of this farm depends on us. It is for *your* sake we drink that milk and eat those apples. Do you know what would happen if we pigs failed in our duty? Jones would come back! Surely, comrades, there is no one among you who wants to see Jones come back?

7 NARRATOR. Now, if there was one thing the animals were completely certain of, it was that they did not want Jones back. When it was put to them in this light they had no more to say. So it was agreed that the milk and the windfall apples . . . and also the main crop of apples when they ripened . . . should be reserved for the pigs alone.

(*Music Cue No. 5.*)

2 SNOWBALL. Every day Snowball and Napoleon sent out flights of pigeons to tell animals on neighboring farms the story of the Rebellion and teach them "Beasts of England."

1 JONES. Most of this time Mr. Jones spent sitting in the taproom of the Red Lion Inn, complaining to anyone who would listen of the monstrous injustice he had suffered. The other farmers didn't give him much help. Each was secretly wondering how he could turn Jones' misfortune to his own advantage.

5 PILKINGTON. The owners of the two farms which adjoined Animal Farm were on permanently bad terms. One of the farms, named Foxwood, was a large, neglected, old-fashioned place much overgrown by woodland. Its owner, Mr. Pilkington, was an easy-going gentleman farmer who spent most of his time fishing or hunting.

3 FREDERICK. The other farm, Pinchfield, was smaller and better kept. Its owner was a Mr. Frederick, a tough, shrewd man with a name for driving hard bargains.

1 NARRATOR. These two disliked each other so much that it was difficult for them to come to any agreement. But they were both thoroughly frightened by the rebellion on Animal Farm, and anxious to prevent their own animals from learning too much about it.

7 NARRATOR. At first they pretended to scorn the idea of animals managing a farm for themselves. The whole thing would be over in a fortnight, they said. They put it about that the animals were perpetually fighting amongst themselves, and were also rapidly starving to death. But as time passed, and the animals had evidently not starved to death, Frederick and Pilkington changed their tune and began to talk about the terrible wickedness that flourished on Animal Farm. It was given out that the animals there practised cannibalism, tortured one another with red-hot horseshoes . . . and had their females in common!

4 NARRATOR. However, these stories were never fully believed. Rumors of a wonderful farm where animals managed their own affairs continued to circulate, and a wave of rebelliousness ran through the countryside. Bulls which had always been tractable suddenly turned savage, sheep broke down hedges and devoured the clover, cows kicked over the pail. Above all, the words and tune of "Beasts of England" were known everywhere. The blackbirds whistled it in the hedges, the pigeons cooed it in the elms; it got into the din of the smithies and the chime of the church bells. And when the human beings listened to it they secretly trembled, hearing in it a prophecy of their future doom.

1 JONES. Early in October a flight of pigeons came whirling through the air to alight in the yard of Animal Farm in the wildest excitement. Jones and his men were entering the gate! They were all carrying sticks, except Jones, who was marching ahead with a gun in his hands.

Obviously they were going to attempt to recapture the farm.

2 SNOWBALL. Snowball, who had studied an old book of Julius Caesar's campaigns, gave orders quickly, and in a couple of minutes every animal was at his post. As the human beings approached the farm buildings, Snowball launched his first attack. All the pigeons flew over the men's heads and muted on them from midair, and while the men were dealing with this, the geese rushed out and pecked viciously at their legs. However, the men easily drove the geese off with their sticks.

4 NARRATOR. Snowball now launched his second line of attack. Muriel, Benjamin, and all the sheep, with Snowball at their head, rushed forward and prodded and butted the men, while Benjamin turned round and lashed at them with his hoofs. But once again the men were too strong for them. Suddenly, at a squeal from Snowball, all the animals turned and fled through the gateway into the yard.

1 JONES. The men gave a shout of triumph. They saw, as they imagined, their enemies in flight, and rushed after them in disorder.

2 SNOWBALL. This was exactly what Snowball had intended. As soon as they were inside the yard, the horses, the cows, and the rest of the pigs, who had been lying in ambush in the cowshed, suddenly emerged in their rear. Snowball gave the signal for the charge. He himself dashed straight for Jones.

1 JONES. Jones raised his gun and fired. The pellets scored bloody streaks along Snowball's back . . . and a sheep dropped dead.

2 SNOWBALL. Snowball flung himself against Jones' legs. Jones was hurled into a pile of dung, and his gun flew out of his hands.

5 BOXER. Most terrifying spectacle was Boxer rearing up on his hind legs and striking out with his great iron-shod hoofs like a stallion. His very first blow took a stableboy on the skull and stretched him lifeless in the mud.

1 JONES. At this sight, several men dropped their at-

tack and tried to run. Panic overtook them, and the next moment all the animals were chasing them round and round the yard. They were gored, kicked, bitten, trampled on. Within five minutes of the invasion they were in ignominious retreat, with a flock of geese hissing after them.

6 NAPOLEON. The animals reassembled in wildest excitement, each recounting his own exploits in the battle at the top of his voice. An impromptu celebration of the victory was held immediately. "Beasts of England" was sung a number of times, and the sheep who had been killed was given a solemn funeral. Napoleon made a little speech, emphasizing the need of all animals to be ready to die for Animal Farm if need be.

1 NARRATOR. The animals decided unanimously to create a military decoration, Animal Hero First Class, consisting of a brass medal to be worn on Sundays and holidays. It was conferred then and there on Snowball and Boxer.

2 BENJAMIN. There was also Animal Hero Second Class, which was conferred posthumously on the dead sheep.

1 NARRATOR. There was much discussion as to what the battle should be called. In the end, it was named the Battle of the Cowshed, since that was where the ambush had taken place. Mr. Jones' gun was set up at the foot of the flagstaff to be fired twice a year: once on the anniversary of the Battle of the Cowshed, and once on the anniversary of the Rebellion.

(*Music Cue No. 6.*)

7 MOLLIE. As winter drew on, Mollie became more and more troublesome. She was late for work every morning, and complained of mysterious pains, though her appetite was excellent. One day Clover took her aside.

4 CLOVER. Mollie, I have something very serious to say to you. This morning I saw you looking over the hedge that divides Animal Farm from Foxwood. One of

Mr. Pilkington's men was on the other side of the hedge, and you were allowing him to stroke your nose. What does this mean, Mollie?

7 MOLLIE. He didn't! I wasn't! It isn't true!

4 CLOVER. Mollie, look me in the face. Do you give me your word of honor that man was not stroking your nose?

7 MOLLIE. It isn't true!

1 NARRATOR. But she could not look Clover in the face, and the next moment she took to her heels and galloped away. For some weeks nothing was known of her whereabouts. Then some pigeons reported they had seen her between the shafts of a smart dog-cart standing outside a public house. A fat, red-faced man was stroking her nose and feeding her sugar. Her coat was newly clipped, and she wore a scarlet ribbon round her forelock. None of the animals ever mentioned Mollie again.

2 SNOWBALL. In January the earth was like iron, and nothing could be done in the fields. The pigs occupied themselves with planning the work of the coming season. It had come to be accepted that the pigs should decide all questions of farm policy . . . though their decisions had to be ratified by a majority vote. This arrangement would have worked out well had it not been for Snowball and Napoleon. These two disagreed at every point where disagreement was possible. Each had his own following, and there were some violent debates. At the meetings, Snowball often won over the majority by his brilliant speeches . . .

6 NAPOLEON. . . . but Napoleon was better at canvassing support for himself in between times. He was especially successful with the sheep. Snowball often had the greatest difficulty in finishing a speech.

2 SNOWBALL. Comrades, I have something to tell you. . . .

ALL. Four legs good; two legs baaad! Four legs good, two legs baaaad!

2 SNOWBALL. (*Up, over them.*) Nevertheless, Snowball was full of plans for innovations and improvements.

6 NAPOLEON. Napoleon produced no schemes of his own, but said Snowball's would come to nothing, and seemed to be biding his time.

1 NARRATOR. Of all their controversies, none was so bitter as the one that took place over the windmill. In the long pasture was a small knoll, the highest point on the farm. Snowball declared this was just the place for a windmill, which could be made to operate a dynamo.

2 SNOWBALL. Snowball used as his study a shed which had a smooth wooden floor, suitable for drawing on. Gradually his plans grew into a complicated mass of cranks and cog-wheels covering more than half the floor, which the other animals found completely unintelligible, but very impressive. All of them came to look at Snowball's drawings at least once a day.

6 NAPOLEON. Napoleon had declared himself against the windmill from the start. One day he arrived unexpectedly to examine the plans. He walked heavily around the shed, looked closely at every detail, stood for a while contemplating them out of the corner of his eye . . . then suddenly lifted his leg, urinated over the plans, and walked out without uttering a word!

1 NARRATOR. At last the question of whether or not to begin work on the windmill was to be put to the vote. When the animals were assembled, Snowball stood up and set forth his reasons in glowing terms:

2 SNOWBALL. A whole new life opens to us, comrades! A life of ease and luxury. Electricity will operate thrashing machines, ploughs, harrows, reapers and binders, beside supplying every stall with its own electric light, hot and cold running water, and an electric heater!

1 NARRATOR. By the time he had finished speaking there was no doubt as to which way the vote would go. But at this moment Napoleon uttered a high-pitched whimper of a kind no one had ever heard before . . . (6 NAPOLEON, *high-pitched whimper*.) At this there was a terrible baying . . . and nine enormous dogs came bounding into the barn. They dashed straight for Snow-

ball, who sprang from his place barely in time to escape their snapping jaws.

7 NARRATOR. In a flash he was out of the door and they after him. Too amazed to speak, the animals crowded through the door to watch the chase.

2 SNOWBALL. Snowball was racing across the pasture, the dogs close on his heels. Once he slipped, and one of them all but closed his jaws on his tail. But Snowball whisked free just in time, put on an extra spurt, slipped through a hole in the hedge, and was seen no more.

1 NARRATOR. Silent and terrified, the animals crept back into the barn. In a moment the dogs came bounding back. At first no one could imagine where these creatures came from. But the problem was soon solved. They were the puppies Napoleon had taken away and reared privately. Though not yet full-grown, they were as fierce as wolves. They kept close to Napoleon and wagged their tails to him in the same way as the other dogs had been used to do to Mr. Jones. Napoleon now spoke.

6 NAPOLEON. Comrades, hear me! From now on all questions of farm management will be settled by a special committee of pigs over which I, Napoleon, will preside. You will still assemble on Sundays to salute the flag, sing "Beasts of England," and receive your orders for the week. But there will be no more debates.

2 BENJAMIN. Four young porkers in the front row uttered shrill squeals of disapproval, sprang to their feet and began speaking all at once. But the dogs let out deep, menacing growls, and the pigs fell silent.

7 NARRATOR. Afterwards, Squealer was sent around the farm to explain the new arrangement to the others.

3 SQUEALER. Comrades, I trust every animal appreciates the sacrifice Comrade Napoleon has made in taking on this extra labor to himself? No one believes more firmly than Comrade Napoleon that all animals are equal. He would be only too happy to let you make your decisions for yourselves. But suppose you made the *wrong* decisions, comrades? Then where should we be? Suppose

you had decided to follow Snowball who, as we now know, was no better than a criminal?

4 CLOVER. He fought bravely at the Battle of the Cowshed.

3 SQUEALER. Bravery is not enough. Loyalty and obedience are more important. As to the Battle of the Cowshed . . . Snowball's part in it was very much exaggerated. Discipline, comrades . . . iron discipline. That is the watchword. One false step and our enemies will be upon us. Surely, comrades, you do not want Jones back?

1 NARRATOR. Once again this argument was unanswerable. Certainly the animals did not want Jones back. If the holding of debates on Sunday mornings was liable to bring him back, then the debates must stop. Boxer voiced the general feeling.

5 BOXER. If Comrade Napoleon says it, it must be right.

1 NARRATOR. And from then on he adopted the second maxim, "Napoleon is always right," and added it to his private motto, "I will work harder."

7 NARRATOR. On the third Sunday after Snowball's expulsion the animals were surprised to hear Napoleon announce that the windmill *was* to be built after all! That evening Squealer explained to the other animals that Napoleon had never really been opposed to the windmill.

3 SQUEALER. On the contrary, comrades . . . the plans Snowball drew on the floor of the shed were actually stolen from Napoleon. The windmill was, in fact, Napoleon's creation.

5 BOXER. Then why did he speak so strongly against it?

3 SQUEALER. Oh, comrade, that was Comrade Napoleon's cunning! He pretended to oppose the windmill to get rid of that dangerous character, Snowball. Now that Snowball is out of the way, the plan can go through. Strategy, comrades! That is called strategy!

1 NARRATOR. The animals were not certain what the word meant. But Squealer spoke with such assurance and the dogs with him growled so threateningly that they accepted his explanation without further question.

(Music Cue No. 7.)

1 NARRATOR. All that year the animals worked like slaves. Throughout the spring and summer they worked a sixty hour week, and in August Napoleon announced there would be work on Sunday afternoons as well.

6 NAPOLEON. This work will be strictly voluntary, comrades. Strictly voluntary. But any comrade who fails to volunteer will have his rations reduced by half.

7 NARRATOR. The windmill presented unexpected difficulties. There was a good limestone quarry on the farm, but the problem was how to break up the stone without picks and crowbars . . . which no animal could use. Only after some weeks did the idea occur to somebody of utilizing the force of gravity. Huge boulders were lying all over the bed of the quarry. The animals lashed ropes round these, then dragged them up the slope to the top of the quarry, where they were toppled over the edge to shatter to pieces below. Frequently it took a whole day of exhausting labor to drag a single boulder to the top of the quarry.

5 BOXER. Nothing could have been achieved without Boxer. To see him toiling up the slope inch by inch, his breath coming fast, the tips of his hoofs clawing at the ground, and his great sides matted with sweat, filled everyone with admiration. Clover warned him not to overstrain himself but Boxer would not listen. He had made arrangements with the cockerel to call him three-quarters of an hour earlier in the mornings, instead of half an hour. In his spare moments he would go alone to the quarry, collect a load of broken stones, and drag it to the windmill unassisted.

7 NARRATOR. One Sunday morning Napoleon announced a new policy.

6 NAPOLEON. From now on, comrades, Animal Farm will engage in trade with the neighboring farms.

ALL. What! But, Comrade Napoleon . . .

6 NAPOLEON. The needs of the windmill must override

everything else. I am therefore making arrangements to sell a stack of hay and part of this year's wheat crop.

4 CLOVER. But, Comrade Napoleon, this means dealing with *humans!*

6 NAPOLEON. True, comrade. And I have taken care of that. There will be no need for any of you to come in contact with human beings. A Mr. Whymper has agreed to act as intermediary between Animal Farm and the outside world.

1 NARRATOR. Thus, every Monday, Mr. Whymper visited the farm. The animals avoided him as much as possible. Nevertheless, the sight of Napoleon, on all fours, delivering orders to a man who stood on two legs, roused their pride and partly reconciled them to the new arrangement.

7 NARRATOR. It was about this time the pigs suddenly moved into the farmhouse. The animals seemed to remember that a resolution against this had been passed in the early days. But again Squealer was able to convince them this was not the case.

3 SQUEALER. It is absolutely necessary, comrades, that we pigs should have a quiet place to work. It is also more suited to the dignity of Napoleon. Comrades, you would not want to see our noble leader living in a mere *sty,* would you?

1 NARRATOR. Nevertheless, some of the animals were disturbed when they heard that the pigs not only took their meals in the kitchen and used the drawing-room as a recreation room, but also slept in the beds. Boxer passed it off with:

5 BOXER. Napoleon is always right!

1 NARRATOR. But Clover went to the barn and tried to puzzle out the Seven Commandments inscribed there.

4 CLOVER. Muriel, read me the Fourth Commandment. Doesn't it say something about never sleeping in a bed?

1 NARRATOR. With some difficulty, Muriel spelled it out.

7 MURIEL. No, Clover. It says, No animal shall sleep in a bed . . . *with sheets.*

1 NARRATOR. Clover had not remembered that the Commandment mentioned sheets. But since it was written on the wall, it must be so. Squealer was able to put the whole matter in its proper perspective.

3 SQUEALER. You have heard, then, comrades, that we pigs now sleep in the beds at the farmhouse? And why not? A bed is merely a place to sleep in. The rule was against *sheets,* which are a human invention. We have removed the sheets from the beds and sleep between *blankets.* You would not want to rob us of our repose, would you, comrades? Surely none of you wants to see Jones back?

1 NARRATOR. No more was said about the pigs sleeping in the farmhouse beds. And when it was announced that from now on the pigs would get up an hour later in the mornings than the other animals, no complaint was made about that, either.

(*Music Cue No. 8.*)

7 NARRATOR. All this while, no more had been seen of Snowball. He was rumored to be in hiding on one of the neighboring farms: Foxwood or Pinchfield. Now it happened that there was in the yard a pile of timber which both Mr. Pilkington and Mr. Frederick were anxious to buy. Napoleon was hesitating between the two. Whenever he seemed to favor making an agreement with Frederick, Snowball was declared to be hiding at Foxwood . . . while when he was inclined toward Pilkington, Snowball was said to be at Pinchfield.

2 SNOWBALL. Suddenly, early in spring, an alarming thing was reported. Snowball was secretly invading the farm by night! Every night, it was said, he came creeping in under cover of darkness to perform all kinds of mischief. He stole the corn, upset the milk pails, broke the eggs; he trampled the seed-beds; he gnawed the bark off the fruit trees.

6 NAPOLEON. Napoleon decreed a full investigation. With his dogs, he made a careful tour of the farm buildings. In the evening, Squealer had serious news to report.

3 SQUEALER. Comrades, a most terrible thing has been discovered. Snowball has sold himself to Frederick of Pinchfield, who is plotting to attack us!

ALL. Oh, no! No!

3 SQUEALER. Yes! But there is worse than that. Snowball was in league with Jones from the very start! This has been proved by documents which we have just discovered. This explains a great deal, comrades. Did we not see for ourselves how he attempted to get us defeated at the Battle of the Cowshed?

1 NARRATOR. The animals were stupefied. They all remembered . . . or *thought* they remembered . . . Snowball charging ahead of them at the Battle of the Cowshed. It was a little difficult to see how this fitted in with his being on Jones' side.

5 BOXER. I don't understand. Snowball fought bravely at the Battle of the Cowshed. Didn't we give him Animal Hero First Class immediately afterward?

3 SQUEALER. That was our mistake, comrade. We know now that in reality he was trying to lure us to our doom.

5 BOXER. But he was wounded! We all saw him running with blood.

3 SQUEALER. That was part of the plot. Jones' shot only grazed him. The plan was for Snowball, at the critical moment, to give the signal for flight and leave the field to the enemy. And he very nearly succeeded. Comrade, he *would* have succeeded if it had not been for our heroic leader, Comrade Napoleon. Do you not remember how, just at the moment when Jones and his men had got inside the yard, Snowball suddenly turned and fled? And do you not remember, too, that just at that moment, when all seemed lost, Comrade Napoleon sprang forward with a cry of "Death to Humanity!" and sank his teeth in Jones' leg?

1 NARRATOR. Now that Squealer described the scene

so graphically, it seemed to the animals that they *did* remember it. But Boxer was still uneasy.

5 BOXER. I don't believe Snowball was a traitor at the beginning. What he's done since is different. But I believe that at the Battle of the Cowshed he was a good comrade.

3 SQUEALER. Comrade Boxer! Our Leader, Comrade Napoleon, has stated categorically . . . categorically, comrade! . . . that Snowball was Jones' agent from the very beginning!

5 BOXER. Ah, that's different. If Comrade Napoleon says so, it must be right.

3 SQUEALER. That is the true spirit, comrade. I warn every animal on this farm to keep his eyes wide open. We have good reason to suspect that at this very moment some of Snowball's secret agents are lurking amongst us.

7 NARRATOR. Four days later, Napoleon ordered all of the animals to assemble in the yard. When they were all gathered, Napoleon emerged from the farmhouse with his nine dogs frisking around him. He stood sternly surveying his audience for a moment. Then:

6 NAPOLEON. (*Stridently.*) Seize them!

1 NARRATOR. Immediately the dogs seized four of the pigs by the ear and dragged them squealing with terror to Napoleon's feet. The pigs' ears were bleeding . . . the dogs had tasted blood . . . and for a few moments they appeared to go quite mad. To the amazement of everybody, three of them flung themselves upon Boxer!

5 BOXER. Boxer put out his great hoof, caught one dog in mid-air, and pinned him to the ground. The dog shrieked for mercy. Boxer looked at Napoleon to know whether he should crush the dog to death.

6 NAPOLEON. (*Grudgingly.*) Let him go!

5 BOXER. Boxer lifted his hoof, and the dog slunk away. Presently the tumult died. The four pigs waited, trembling. They were the same four who had protested when Napoleon abolished the Sunday meetings.

6 NAPOLEON. Comrades, in the name of the Rebellion I now call upon you to confess your heinous crimes!

7 NARRATOR. Without further prompting the porkers confessed that they had been secretly in touch with Snowball ever since his expulsion, and had entered into an agreement with him to hand over the farm to Mr. Frederick. They added that Snowball had privately admitted to them that he had been Mr. Jones' secret agent for years. When they had finished their confessions, the dogs promptly tore their throats out.

6 NAPOLEON. Has any other animal anything to confess?

1 NARRATOR. Three hens now stated that Snowball had appeared to them in a dream and incited them to disobey Napoleon's orders. Then a goose confessed to having secreted six ears of corn and eaten them in the night. Then a sheep confessed to having urinated in the drinking pool . . . urged to do this by Snowball. They were all slain on the spot.

7 NARRATOR. So the tale of confessions and executions went on and on, until there was a pile of corpses lying before Napoleon's feet, and the air was heavy with the smell of blood. When it was all over, the animals crept away in a body, shaken and miserable. They made their way to the little knoll where the half-finished windmill stood. Boxer seemed bewildered by it all.

5 BOXER. I do not understand. I wouldn't have believed such things could happen on our farm. It must be some fault in ourselves. The solution, as I see it, is to work harder. From now on I will get up a whole hour earlier in the mornings.

1 NARRATOR. And Boxer made for the quarry. The other animals huddled about Clover, not speaking. The knoll where they were lying gave them a wide prospect across the countryside. Most of Animal Farm was within their view . . . the long pasture stretching down to the main road, the hayfield, the spinney, the drinking pool, the ploughed fields where the young wheat was thick and green, and the red roofs of the farm buildings with smoke

curling from the chimneys. It was a clear spring evening. The grass and the bursting hedges were gilded by the level rays of the sun. Never had the farm appeared to the animals so desirable. As Clover looked down the hillside, her eyes filled with tears.

4 CLOVER. But surely this is not what we looked forward to on that night when old Major first stirred us to rebellion? He told of a society of animals set free from hunger and the whip . . . all equal, each working according to his capacity, the strong protecting the weak. What has happened to us? We have come to a time when no one dares speak his mind; when fierce, growling dogs roam everywhere; when you have to watch your comrades torn to pieces after confessing to shocking crimes. Oh, things are far better off than in the days of Jones. And before all else it is needful to prevent the return of the human beings. But still it was not for *this* that we have hoped and toiled. It was not for *this* we faced the bullets of Jones' gun.

1 NARRATOR. Such were Clover's thoughts, though she lacked the words to express them. At last, feeling it to be in some way a substitute for the words they were unable to find, the animals began singing "Beasts of England" . . .

ALL. (*Softly.*)
> Beasts of England, beasts of Ireland,
> Beasts of every land and clime,
> Hearken to my joyful tidings
> Of the golden future time.

(*Sing until stopped by* SQUEALER.)

1 NARRATOR. (*Over them.*) They sang it slowly and mournfully in a way they had never sung it before . . . until suddenly Squealer appeared.

3 SQUEALER. Stop! Comrades, hear me! Stop singing that song. "Beasts of England" has been abolished. From now on it is forbidden to sing it.

ALL. What! But *why?*

3 SQUEALER. Because it is no longer needed. "Beasts of England" was the song of the Rebellion. But the Rebellion is now completed. The execution of the traitors this afternoon was the final act. In "Beasts of England" we expressed our longing for a better society to come. Now that society has been established. Clearly this song no longer has any purpose. We have a new song which I shall now teach you. (*Sings.*)

Animal Farm, Animal Farm,

Never through me shalt thou come to harm . . .

7 NARRATOR. The new anthem was sung every Sunday morning after the hoisting of the flag. But somehow neither the words nor the tune ever seemed to the animals to come up to "Beasts of England."

(*Music Cue No. 9.*)

THE CURTAIN FALLS

END OF ACT I

ACT II

The readers return to their stools during the playing of Music Cue No. 10, which is faded out under:

1 NARRATOR. A few days later, when the terror caused by the executions had died down, some of the animals thought they remembered that the Sixth Commandment decreed no animal should kill any other animal. It was felt that the killings which had taken place did not square with this.

4 CLOVER. Clover asked Benjamin to read her the Sixth Commandment . . .

2 BENJAMIN. Not I! Nobody has ever seen a dead donkey.

4 CLOVER. . . . and when Benjamin refused to meddle in such matters, she fetched Muriel to read the Commandment for her.

7 MURIEL. No animal shall kill any other animal . . . *without cause.*

1 NARRATOR. Somehow or other these last two words had slipped everyone's memory. But they saw now that the Commandment had not been violated, for clearly there was good reason for killing the traitors who had leagued themselves with Snowball.

5 BOXER. Throughout that year the animals worked even harder than the previous year. At times it seemed they worked longer hours and fed no better than in Jones' day. But on Sunday mornings, Squealer would read them long, reassuring lists of figures.

3 SQUEALER. Production Report for the week just completed: Hay production, up 200 percent . . . grains, 300 percent . . . milk, 400 percent . . . eggs, five hundred and six point two percent.

7 NARRATOR. The animals saw no reason to disbelieve these impressive figures. All the same, Benjamin expressed the general sentiment when he said:

2 BENJAMIN. I'd rather have less figures and more food!

6 NAPOLEON. All orders were now issued through Squealer. Napoleon himself was not seen in public once in a fortnight. Even in the farmhouse Napoleon inhabited separate apartments, took his meals alone, and always ate from the Crown Derby dinner service. It was also announced that the gun would be fired every year on Napoleon's birthday, as well as on the other two anniversaries.

1 NARRATOR. Napoleon was now always referred to in formal style as Our Leader, Comrade Napoleon, and the pigs liked to invent for him such titles as Father of All Animals, Protector of the Sheepfold, Ducklings' Friend, and the like. In his speeches, Squealer would talk with the tears running down his cheeks of Napoleon's wisdom, the goodness of his heart, and the deep love he bore to all animals everywhere. It had become customary to give Napoleon the credit for every successful achievement. You would often hear one hen remark to another:

4 ANIMAL. Under the guidance of Our Leader, Comrade Napoleon, I have laid five eggs in six days.

1 NARRATOR. Or two cows, drinking at a pool, would exclaim:

7 ANIMAL. Thanks to the leadership of Comrade Napoleon, how excellent this water tastes!

1 NARRATOR. Meanwhile, Napoleon was engaged in complicated negotiations with Frederick and Pilkington. The pile of timber was still unsold. Frederick was the more anxious to get hold of it, but he would not offer a reasonable price. At the same time there were renewed rumors that Frederick and his men were plotting to attack Animal Farm and destroy the windmill.

3 SQUEALER. Frederick plots to bring against us twenty men, all armed with guns. And, comrades, have you heard about the terrible cruelties Frederick practises on his animals? He flogged an old horse to death . . . he starves his cows . . . he killed his dog by throwing it into the furnace . . . he amuses himself in the evenings

by making cocks fight with splinters of razor blade tied to their spurs!

1 NARRATOR. The animals' blood boiled with rage when they heard of these things, and sometimes they clamored to be allowed to attack Pinchfield Farm and set the animals free.

6 NAPOLEON. Napoleon explained that he had never contemplated selling the timber to Frederick. The pigeons, who were still sent out to spread tidings of the Rebellion, were forbidden to set foot on Pinchfield, and were ordered to drop their former slogan of "Death to Humanity" in favor of "Death to Frederick."

2 SNOWBALL. In the late summer, yet another of Snowball's machinations was laid bare. The wheat crop was full of weeds, and it was discovered that on one of his nocturnal visits Snowball had mixed weed seeds with the seed corn. A gander who had been privy to the plot confessed his guilt, and immediately committed suicide by swallowing deadly nightshade berries.

4 CLOVER. The animals now also learned that Snowball had never received the order of Animal Hero First Class, as many of them had believed.

3 SQUEALER. This was merely a legend circulated by Snowball himself. Far from being decorated, he was actually censured for cowardice in the battle!

7 NARRATOR. By autumn the windmill was finished. Tired but proud, the animals walked round and round their masterpiece, which appeared beautiful in their eyes. When they thought of how they had labored, what discouragements they had overcome, and the enormous difference that would be made in their lives when the sails were turning and the dynamos running, their weariness forsook them and they gambolled round and round the windmill uttering cries of triumph. Napoleon himself came to inspect the completed work, congratulated the animals on their achievement, and dedicated the edifice.

6 NAPOLEON. I hereby name this structure . . . Napoleon Mill!

1 NARRATOR. Two days later the animals were struck

dumb with surprise to learn that Napoleon had sold the pile of timber to Frederick. Throughout the whole of his seeming friendship with Pilkington, he had really been in secret agreement with Frederick!

7 NARRATOR. The pigs were in ecstasies over Napoleon's cunning. By seeming to be friendly with Pilkington, he had forced Frederick to raise his price by twelve pounds. Squealer gloated:

3 SQUEALER. Comrades, the superior quality of Napoleon's mind is shown in the fact that he trusted *nobody.* Frederick wanted to pay for the timber with something he called a cheque. But Our Leader was too clever for him. He demanded payment in real five pound notes, to be handed over before the timber is removed.

1 NARRATOR. Frederick removed the timber with amazing speed. But three days later there was a terrible hullabaloo. Whymper, his face deadly pale, came racing up the path on his bicycle and rushed straight to the farmhouse. The next moment the animals heard a choking roar of rage from Napoleon's apartment.

6 NAPOLEON. (*Outraged scream.*) Death! Death to Frederick!

1 NARRATOR. News of what had happened spread around the farm like wildfire. The banknotes were forgeries! Frederick had got the timber for nothing!

7 NARRATOR. Napoleon called the animals together, and in a terrible voice pronounced judgment on Frederick.

6 NAPOLEON. When captured, he shall be boiled alive!

7 NARRATOR. At the same time, he warned them that after this treacherous deed, Frederick and his men might make their long-expected attack at any moment. Four pigeons were sent to Foxwood with a conciliatory message which it was hoped might re-establish good relations with Pilkington.

1 NARRATOR. The very next morning the attack came. The lookouts came racing in with the news that Frederick and his men had come through the gate. Boldly the animals sallied forth to meet them. But this time they did not have the easy victory they had had in the Battle of

the Cowshed. There were fifteen men with half a dozen guns, and they opened fire as soon as they got within fifty yards.

7 NARRATOR. The animals took refuge in the farm buildings and peeped cautiously out from chinks and knotholes. The whole of the big pasture, including the windmill, was in the hands of the enemy.

6 NAPOLEON. Napoleon seemed at a loss. He paced up and down, casting wistful glances in the direction of Foxwood. If Pilkington and his men would help, the day might yet be won. But at this moment the pigeons returned bearing a scrap of paper.

3 SQUEALER. A message from Pilkington, Comrade Napoleon!

6 NAPOLEON. Quickly, what does it say?

4 CLOVER. Is he coming?

5 BOXER. Will he help us?

6 NAPOLEON. What does it say?

3 SQUEALER. It says . . . "Serves you right!"

1 NARRATOR. Frederick and his men halted at the windmill. Two of the men produced a crowbar and a sledge hammer. The animals watched them, and a murmur of dismay went round.

7 MURIEL. They are going to knock the windmill down!

6 NAPOLEON. Impossible! The walls are too thick. They could not knock it down in a week. Courage, comrades.

1 NARRATOR. But the men were drilling a hole in the base of the windmill. Slowly, and with an air almost of amusement, Benjamin nodded his long muzzle.

2 BENJAMIN. I thought so. Do you see what they're doing? They're packing blasting powder into that hole.

1 NARRATOR. In a few minutes there was a sudden deafening roar. All the animals flung themselves flat on their faces. When they got up again, a huge cloud of smoke was hanging where the windmill had been. Slowly the breeze drifted it away. (*All ad lib moans of distress.*) The windmill had ceased to exist. At this sight the animals' fear and despair were drowned in their rage against

this vile, contemptible act. (*All ad lib roars of fury.*) A mighty cry of vengeance went up, and without waiting for orders from Napoleon, they charged forth in a body and made straight for the enemy. This time they did not heed the cruel pellets that swept them like hail. It was a savage and bitter battle. A cow, three sheep and two geese were killed, and nearly everyone was wounded . . . except Napoleon, who was directing operations from the rear.

7 NARRATOR. The men did not go unscathed, either. Two of them had their heads broken by blows from Boxer's hoofs; another was gored in the belly by a cow's horn. And when the nine dogs suddenly appeared on the men's flank, baying ferociously, the cowardly enemy turned and ran for dear life. The animals chased them right down to the bottom of the field and got in some last kicks at them as they forced their way through the thorn hedge.

5 BOXER. Weary and bleeding, the animals began to limp back to the farm. They halted in sorrowful silence at the place where the windmill had once stood. It was gone. Almost the last trace of their labor was gone. It was as though the windmill had never been.

3 SQUEALER. But as they approached the farm, Squealer, who had unaccountably been absent during the fight, came skipping towards them, beaming. From the direction of the farm buildings the animals heard the solemn firing of a gun.

2 BENJAMIN. What is that gun firing for?

3 SQUEALER. To celebrate our victory.

2 BENJAMIN. Victory! *What* victory?

3 SQUEALER. What victory, comrade! Have we not driven the enemy off the sacred soil of Animal Farm?

2 BENJAMIN. But they have destroyed the windmill!

3 SQUEALER. What matter? We will build *another* windmill. We'll build *six* windmills if we feel like it. You do not appreciate, comrade, the mighty thing we have done. The enemy was in occupation of the very ground we

stand on. Now, thanks to the leadership of Comrade Napoleon, we have won back every inch of it.

2 BENJAMIN. Then we've won back what we had before.

3 SQUEALER. *That* is our victory!

5 BOXER. Boxer, who had suffered a split hoof, limped painfully back into the yard. He saw ahead of him the heavy labor of rebuilding the windmill from its foundations, and already in imagination braced himself for the task. But for the first time it occurred to him that he was eleven years old, and his great muscles were not what they once had been.

1 NARRATOR. But when the animals heard Napoleon's speech, congratulating them on their conduct, it *did* seem to them that, after all, they *had* won a great victory. The animals slain in the battle were given a solemn funeral. It was announced that the battle would be called the Battle of the Windmill.

2 BENJAMIN. And Napoleon created a new decoration, the Order of the Green Banner . . . which he conferred upon himself.

7 NARRATOR. A few days later, the pigs came upon a case of whisky in the cellar of the farmhouse, overlooked when the house was first occupied. That night there came from the farmhouse the sound of raucous singing. At about half past nine, Napoleon, wearing an old bowler hat of Mr. Jones', was distinctly seen to emerge from the back door, gallop rapidly around the yard, and disappear indoors again.

1 NARRATOR. But in the morning a deep silence hung over the farmhouse. Not a pig appeared to be stirring. It was nearly nine o'clock before Squealer made his appearance, walking slowly and dejectedly, his eyes dull, with every appearance of being seriously ill. He called the animals together and told them he had terrible news to impart.

3 SQUEALER. Comrades . . . Comrade Napoleon is dying!

1 NARRATOR. A cry of lamentation went up. With tears

in their eyes the animals asked one another what they should do if their Leader were taken from them. A rumor went round that Snowball had contrived to *poison* Napoleon. At eleven o'clock Squealer came to make another announcement.

3 SQUEALER. As his last act on earth, Comrade Napoleon has pronounced a solemn decree . . . the drinking of alcohol is to be punished by death!

6 NAPOLEON. By evening, however, Napoleon appeared to be somewhat better. The following morning Squealer was able to tell them he was well on his way to recovery. And the next day it was learned that he had instructed Whymper to purchase some books on brewing and distilling. The small paddock beyond the orchard was to be ploughed up. Napoleon intended to sow it with barley.

1 NARRATOR. About this time occurred a strange incident. One night there was a loud crash in the yard, and the animals rushed out of their stalls. At the foot of the end wall of the big barn, where the Seven Commandments were written, lay a ladder broken in two. Squealer was sprawling beside it, and near at hand lay a lantern, a paint brush, and an overturned pot of white paint. None of the animals could form any idea what this meant, except old Benjamin, who nodded his muzzle with a knowing air and would say nothing.

7 MURIEL. But a few days later, Muriel, reading over the Seven Commandments to herself, noticed there was yet *another* of them which the animals had remembered wrong. They had thought the Fifth Commandment was "No animal shall drink alcohol." But there were two words they had forgotten. Actually the Commandment read, "No animal shall drink alcohol . . . *to excess!*"

(Music Cue No. 11.)

5 BOXER. Boxer's split hoof was a long time healing. They had started rebuilding the windmill the day after the victory celebration. Boxer refused to take even a day off, and made it a point of honor not to let it be seen that

he was in pain. Clover treated the hoof with poultices, and both she and Benjamin urged Boxer to work less hard, but he would not listen. He had one burning ambition: to see the windmill completed before he reached the age for retirement.

1 NARRATOR. At the beginning, the retirement age had been fixed for horses and pigs at twelve, for cows at fourteen, for dogs at nine, sheep at seven, for hens and geese at five. So far no animal had actually retired. But now that the small field beyond the orchard had been planted in barley, it was rumored that a corner of the large pasture was to be turned into a grazing ground for superannuated animals. Boxer's twelfth birthday was due in the summer of the next year.

7 NARRATOR. Meanwhile, life was hard. The winter was as cold as the last one, and food was even shorter. Once again all rations were reduced . . . except those of the pigs and the dogs. Squealer explained.

3 SQUEALER. We are not *really* short of food, comrades. In comparison with the days of Jones the improvement is tremendous. We have more oats, more hay, more turnips. We work shorter hours, our drinking water is of better quality, we live longer, have more straw in our stalls . . . and suffer less from fleas.

7 NARRATOR. The animals believed every word of it. Truth to tell, Jones and all that he stood for had almost faded out of their memories.

1 NARRATOR. In the autumn, the four sows all littered simultaneously, producing thirty-one young pigs. It was announced that a schoolroom would be built in the farmhouse garden. For the time being, the young pigs were to be given their instruction by Napoleon himself. They were discouraged from playing with the other young animals. It was laid down as a rule that when a pig and any other animal met on a path, the other animal must stand aside. Also, all pigs now enjoyed the privilege of wearing green ribbons in their tails on Sundays.

2 BENJAMIN. The farm was still short of money. There were bricks, sand and lime for the schoolroom to be pur-

chased, and it was also necessary to begin saving up again for machinery for the windmill. Rations, reduced in December, were reduced again in February. Lanterns in the stalls were forbidden to save oil. But the pigs seemed comfortable enough and, in fact, were putting on weight, if anything. The news leaked out that every pig was now receiving a ration of a pint of beer daily, with half a gallon for Napoleon himself, which was always served to him in a Crown Derby tureen.

1 NARRATOR. But if there were hardships to be borne, they were partly offset by the fact that life nowadays had greater dignity than ever before. There were more songs, more speeches, more processions. So what with Squealer's lists of figures and the fluttering of the flag, the animals were able to forget . . . at least part of the time . . . that their bellies were empty.

7 NARRATOR. In April, Animal Farm was proclaimed a republic, and it became necessary to elect a President. There was only one candidate, Napoleon. He was elected unanimously. On the same day it was given out that fresh documents had been discovered which revealed further details about Snowball's complicity with Jones. It now appeared that Snowball had not merely attempted to *lose* the Battle of the Cowshed, but had openly been fighting on Jones' side! In fact, he had actually been the *leader* of the human forces, charging into battle with the cry, "Long Live Humanity!" on his lips. The wounds on Snowball's back, which a few of the animals still remembered seeing, had been inflicted by Napoleon's teeth.

1 NARRATOR. In the middle of the summer, Moses the raven suddenly reappeared on the farm. He was quite unchanged, still did no work, and would still talk by the hour to anyone who would listen about:

3 MOSES. Sugarcandy Mountain, comrades! Oh, beautiful, glorious Sugarcandy Mountain . . . up there, up there, comrades, just on the other side of that dark and dismal cloud. That happy land where we poor animals shall rest forever from our labors. Oh, I've been there, brethren . . . I've seen it! The everlasting fields of clover

. . . the linseed cake and lump sugar growing on the hedges. Oh, it's beautiful, comrades . . . beautiful!

1 NARRATOR. Many of the animals believed him. Was it not right and just that somewhere a better world should exist? A thing difficult to comprehend was the attitude of the pigs toward Moses. They declared contemptuously that his stories about Sugarcandy Mountain were lies . . . yet they allowed him to remain on the farm, not working, with an allowance of a gill of beer a day.

5 BOXER. After his hoof healed, Boxer worked harder than ever. Sometimes the long hours on insufficient food were hard to bear, but Boxer never faltered. In nothing he said or did was there any sign that his strength was not what it had been. It was only his appearance that was a little altered . . . his hide less shiny than it used to be, and his great haunches seemed to have shrunken. Sometimes on the slope leading to the top of the quarry, when he braced his great muscles against the weight of some vast boulder, it seemed that nothing kept him on his feet except the will to continue. Clover and Benjamin begged him to take care of his health, but Boxer paid no attention. Late one evening in summer, two pigeons came racing in with dreadful news.

2 ANIMAL. Boxer has fallen!

7 ANIMAL. He is lying on his side and can't get up!

1 NARRATOR. The animals rushed to the knoll where the windmill stood. There lay Boxer, his neck stretched out, unable even to raise his head. His eyes were glazed, his sides matted with sweat, and a thin stream of blood had trickled out of his mouth. Clover dropped to her knees beside him.

4 CLOVER. Boxer, what is it? What's wrong?

5 BOXER. It's . . . my lung. No matter. You will be able to finish the windmill without me. I had only a month to go, in any case. To tell you the truth, I have been looking forward to my retirement.

2 BENJAMIN. We must get help at once. Run, somebody, and tell Squealer what has happened!

1 NARRATOR. About a quarter of an hour later Squealer appeared, full of sympathy and concern.

3 SQUEALER. Comrade Napoleon has learned with the deepest distress of this misfortune to one of our most loyal workers. He has already made arrangements to send Boxer to the town hospital for treatment.

7 NARRATOR. The animals felt a little uneasy at this. They did not like to think of their sick comrade in the hands of human beings. However, Squealer convinced them that the veterinary surgeon could treat Boxer more satisfactorily than could be done on the farm. And about a half hour later, when Boxer had somewhat recovered, he managed to limp back to his stall.

5 BOXER. I'm not too sorry about what's happened. Why, if I make a good recovery I might expect to live another three years. I look forward to the peaceful days I will spend in the corner of the big pasture.

4 CLOVER. But, Boxer . . . what will you ever do with your spare time?

5 BOXER. I have a plan. Something I've long wanted to do.

4 CLOVER. What is it, Boxer?

5 BOXER. I'm going to devote the rest of my life to learning the remaining 22 letters of the alphabet.

1 NARRATOR. In the middle of the day a van came to take him away. The animals were at work when Benjamin came galloping from the direction of the farm buildings, braying at the top of his voice. It was the first time they had ever seen Benjamin excited.

2 BENJAMIN. Quick! Quick! Come at once! They're taking Boxer away!

1 NARRATOR. The animals raced back to the farm buildings. Sure enough, there in the yard stood a large closed van with a sly looking man sitting on the driver's seat. The animals crowded round the van.

6 ANIMAL. There he is, inside!

7 ANIMAL. He's going away.

3 & 4 ANIMALS. (*Fatuously cheerful.*) Goodbye, Boxer! Goodbye!

2 BENJAMIN. Fools! Fools! Don't you see what's written on the side of that van?

4 CLOVER. (*Slowly, with mounting horror.*) Alfred Simmonds . . . Horse Slaughterer and Glue Boiler!

2 BENJAMIN. Don't you understand what that means? They're selling Boxer to the knacker!

(*All ad lib cries of horror and rejection.*)

4 CLOVER. Stop him, somebody! Stop him!

3 ANIMAL. Come back here!

2 BENJAMIN. Boxer, get out! Get out, quickly! They're taking you to your death!

5 BOXER. They heard the sound of a tremendous drumming of hoofs from inside the van. But the van was already gathering speed. In another moment it disappeared down the road. Boxer was never seen again.

7 NARRATOR. Three days later it was announced that he had died in the hospital in spite of receiving every attention a horse could have. Squealer came to announce the news to the others.

3 SQUEALER. I was at his bedside at the very last. At the end, almost too weak to speak, he whispered in my ear that his sole sorrow was to have passed on before the windmill was finished. "Forward, comrades!" he whispered. "Forward in the name of the Rebellion! Long live Animal Farm! Long live Napoleon!" Those were his very last words, comrades.

7 NARRATOR. The animals were enormously impressed. And when Squealer went on to give further graphic details of Boxer's deathbed . . . the admirable care he had received, and the expensive medicines for which Napoleon had paid without a thought as to the cost . . . the sorrow they felt for their comrade's death was tempered by the thought that at least he had died happy.

1 NARRATOR. Napoleon himself appeared at the meeting the following Sunday morning and pronounced a short oration in Boxer's honor.

6 NAPOLEON. We deeply regret that it was not possible

to bring back our late lamented comrade's remains for interment on the farm. But in a few days the pigs intend to hold a memorial banquet in Boxer's honor. Meanwhile, let me remind you of his priceless heritage to us: two maxims which every animal would do well to adopt as his own. Remember forever, comrades, the wise words of our dear Boxer . . . "I will work harder!" . . . and "Comrade Napoleon is always right!"

1 NARRATOR. On the day appointed for the banquet, a grocer delivered a large wooden crate to the farmhouse. That night there was the sound of uproarious singing from within. No one stirred in the farmhouse until noon the following day. From somewhere or other the pigs had acquired the money to buy themselves another case of whisky.

(Music Cue No. 12.)

7 NARRATOR. Years passed. A time came when there was no one who remembered the old days before the Rebellion except Clover, Benjamin, Moses, and a few of the pigs.

2 BENJAMIN. Muriel was dead. Jones had died in an inebriates' home in another part of the country. Snowball was forgotten. Boxer was forgotten . . . except by the few who had loved him. Clover was an old, stout mare now, two years past the retiring age . . . but in fact no animal had ever actually retired. Napoleon was now a mature boar of 24 stone. Squealer was so fat that he could with difficulty see out of his eyes. Only old Benjamin was much the same as ever, except for being a little grayer about the muzzle and, since Boxer's death, more taciturn than ever.

1 NARRATOR. Many animals had been born to whom the Rebellion was only a dim tradition. The farm was more prosperous now, and better organized. The windmill had been successfully completed at last, and the farm possessed a threshing-machine and a hay elevator, and various new buildings.

7 NARRATOR. The windmill had not, after all, been used for generating electrical power. It was used for milling corn, and brought in a handsome profit. But the luxuries of which Snowball had taught the animals to dream . . . the stalls with electric lights, and hot and cold running water . . . these were no longer talked about. Napoleon had denounced such ideas as being contrary to the spirit of Animalism. True happiness, he said, lay in working hard and living frugally.

2 BENJAMIN. Somehow it seemed the farm had grown richer without making the animals themselves any richer. Except, of course, for the pigs and the dogs. It wasn't that these creatures didn't work . . . after their fashion. There was, as Squealer never tired of explaining, endless work in the supervision and organization of the farm.

3 SQUEALER. We pigs have to expend enormous labor every day on things called files, reports and memoranda. These are large sheets of paper which have to be closely covered with writing . . . and as soon as they are so covered, must be burnt in the furnace. This is of the highest importance for the welfare of the farm!

2 BENJAMIN. As for the others, they were generally hungry; they slept on straw; they labored in the fields. In winter they were troubled by the cold, and in summer by the flies. Sometimes the older ones among them racked their dim memories and tried to determine whether in the early days of the Rebellion things had been better or worse. But they could not remember. Squealer's lists of figures invariably demonstrated that everything was getting better and better. Only old Benjamin professed to know that things never had been, nor ever could be, much better or much worse. Hunger, hardship and disappointment were, he said, the unalterable law of life.

4 CLOVER. Yet the animals never gave up hope. They were still the only farm in all England owned and operated by animals. And when they heard the gun booming, and saw the flag fluttering at the masthead, their hearts swelled with pride, and the talk would turn to the old, heroic days . . . the expulsion of Jones, the writing of

the Seven Commandments, the great battles in which the human invaders had been defeated. None of the old dreams had been abandoned. The republic of animals which old Major had foretold was still believed in. If they went hungry, it was not from feeding tyrannical human beings. If they worked hard, at least they worked for themselves. No creature amongst them went on two legs. No creature called any other creature Master. All animals were equal!

3 SQUEALER. One day in early summer, Squealer ordered the sheep to follow him to a piece of waste ground at the other end of the farm. There they remained for a whole week, during which time Squealer was with them for the greater part of every day, teaching them to sing a new song.

4 CLOVER. It was just after the sheep had returned, on a pleasant evening when the animals had finished work and were making their way back to the farm buildings, that a terrified neighing sounded from the yard. It was Clover. She neighed again, and all the animals rushed into the yard. Then *they* saw what Clover had seen.

1 ANIMAL. It . . . it's Squealer!

5 ANIMAL He's walking!

2 ANIMAL. On his hind legs!

3 SQUEALER. Yes, it was Squealer, walking on his hind legs. A little awkwardly, as though not quite used to supporting his considerable bulk in that position, but with perfect balance he was strolling across the yard. And a moment later, out from the farmhouse came a long file of pigs . . . all walking on their hind legs. One or two looked as though they would have liked the support of a stick. But every one of them made his way round the yard successfully.

6 NAPOLEON. Finally there was a tremendous baying of dogs, and out came Napoleon himself, majestically upright, casting haughty glances from side to side, with his dogs gambolling about him. And in his trotter . . . he carried a whip!

1 NARRATOR. There was a deadly silence. Amazed, ter-

rified, the animals watched the long line of pigs march slowly round the yard. It was as though the world had turned upside down. Then came a moment when in spite of everything, in spite of their terror of the dogs, and of the habit developed through long years of never complaining, never criticising, they might have uttered some word of protest. But just at that moment . . . as though at a signal . . . all the sheep burst into a tremendous bleating:

ALL. Four legs good; two legs *better!* Four legs good; two legs *better!*

1 NARRATOR. It went on for five minutes without stopping. And by the time the sheep had quieted down, the pigs had marched back into the farmhouse.

2 BENJAMIN. Benjamin felt a nose nuzzling at his shoulder. It was Clover. She tugged gently at his mane and led him to the end of the big barn where the Seven Commandments were written.

4 CLOVER. My sight is failing. But it appears to me that the wall looks different. Are the Seven Commandments the same as they used to be, Benjamin?

1 NARRATOR. For once, Benjamin consented to break his rule, and he read out to her what was written on the wall. There was nothing there now except a single commandment. It read:

2 BENJAMIN. All animals are equal. But some animals are more equal than others.

1 NARRATOR. After that, it did not seem strange when next day the pigs all carried whips. It did not seem strange to learn the pigs had bought themselves a wireless set, were arranging to install a telephone, and had taken out subscriptions to the daily papers. It did not seem strange when Napoleon was seen strolling in the garden with a pipe in his mouth. . . . No, not even when the pigs took Mr. Jones' clothes out of the wardrobes and put them on.

7 NARRATOR. A week later, a deputation of neighboring farmers came to inspect the farm. They were shown all over, and expressed great admiration for everything they

saw; especially the windmill. The animals worked dil-
igently, hardly raising their faces from the ground, not
knowing whether to be more frightened of the pigs or
of the human visitors. That evening, loud laughter and
bursts of song came from the farmhouse. At the sound
of the mingled voices the animals were stricken with curi-
osity. What could be happening in there, now that for the
first time animals and humans were meeting on terms of
equality? They began to creep quietly into the farmhouse
garden.

1 NARRATOR. They tiptoed up to the house and peered
in the dining-room window. There, round the long table,
sat half a dozen farmers and half a dozen of the more
eminent pigs. Napoleon himself sat at the head of the
table. A large jug was circulating, and the mugs were
being refilled. Mr. Pilkington stood up.

5 PILKINGTON. Mr. Napoleon, ladies, gentlemen . . .
it is a great source of satisfaction to me to feel that a long
period of distrust and misunderstanding has now come to
an end. There was a time when the respected proprietors
of Animal Farm were regarded with a certain amount of
misgiving by their human neighbors. It used to be felt
that the existence of a farm owned and operated by pigs
might have an unsettling effect on the neighborhood. Too
many of us assumed, I fear, that on such a farm a spirit
of license would prevail. We were nervous about the effect
on our own animals. But today we have inspected Animal
Farm . . . and what did we find? Not only the most up-
to-date methods, but a discipline which should be an example to all farmers everywhere. I believe I am right in
saying that on this farm the lower animals do more work
and receive less food than any animals in the country!

3 SQUEALER. Hear, hear!

5 PILKINGTON. Between pigs and human beings there
is not, nor need ever be, any clash of interests whatever.
Our problems are exactly the same. You have your lower
animals to contend with . . . we have our lower classes.
And so, gentlemen, I give you a toast! To the prosperity
of Animal Farm!

(All ad lib applause.)

3 SQUEALER. Thank you, Mr. Pilkington, for those kind remarks. And now our great leader, Napoleon, will say a few words.

6 NAPOLEON. Squealer, honored guests, fellow pigs . . . I, too, am happy that the period of misunderstanding has come to an end. For a long time there were rumors, circulated by a foul and malignant enemy, that there was something subversive . . . even revolutionary . . . in the outlook of myself and my colleagues. We have even been accused of attempting to stir up rebellion among the animals on neighboring farms. Gentlemen, nothing could be farther from the truth! Our sole wish now, as in the past, is to live at peace with everyone.

3 SQUEALER. Hear, hear!

6 NAPOLEON. I do not believe any of the old suspicions still linger. But certain changes recently effected should have the effect of promoting confidence still farther. For example, heretofore the animals on this farm have had the rather foolish custom of addressing each other as "comrade." This is to be discontinued immediately. Moreover, tonight it gives me great pleasure to announce another important change. The name Animal Farm has been abolished. Henceforth this farm is to be known by its correct and original name . . . the Manor Farm. *(All ad lib cheers.)* So, friends, I give you the same toast as before, but in a different form. Fill your glasses to the brim. Gentlemen, here is my toast. To the prosperity of . . . the Manor Farm!

(All ad lib cheers.)

4 CLOVER. There was the same hearty cheering as before, and the mugs were emptied to the dregs. But as the animals outside gazed at the scene, it seemed to them that some strange thing was happening. What *was* it that had altered in the faces of the pigs? Clover's old dim eyes flitted from one face to another. Some of them had five

chins, some had four, some three. But what was it that
seemed to be melting and changing? The creatures outside
looked from pig to man, and from man to pig, and from
pig to man again. But already it was impossible to say
which was which . . .

(Music Cue No. 13 to crashing climax, then:)

THE CURTAIN FALLS

PRODUCTION NOTES

STAGING

Stark simplicity is the keynote for the staging and the lighting pattern of *Animal Farm*. Basic requirements are stools for the readers, and reading stands for their scripts. An attractive elaboration is to mask each of these reading stands with a jet black angled shield, concealing the readers from the waist down.

The position of the stools depends to a great extent on the sightlines from the sides of the audience. They should be spread as much as possible, keeping them apart a minimum distance of 28 inches to avoid spill from lights. Stool #1 is at Stage Right.

LIGHTING

External lighting for *Animal Farm* may be used where facilities permit. Where stage lighting is not available, an inexpensive and interesting variation is to provide each of the reading stands with its individual two-way light switch, controlled by the reader. Each stand is mounted with a tiny 5-watt "holding lamp" and a stronger 25-watt "reading lamp." Whenever a reader "enters the action" he projects himself into the story by switching on his reading lamp; when he is not a participant in the action he removes himself by switching to the holding lamp. The shifting pattern of illumination serves to focus the listeners' attention from one to another stool.